IN THE YEAR 2022, THE GAT

A DEMONIC HORDE INVADES, SLAYING MILLIONS.

THE GLOBAL ECONOMY COLLAPSES.

THOSE WHO SURVIVE EITHER LIVE IN FEAR,

OR PLEDGE ALLEGIANCE TO THE DARK LORD.

A DECREPIT ARMY OF ANGELS, ALONG WITH A LOST ORDER

OF HOLY KNIGHTS, STAND AGAINST THE ARMIES OF EVIL.

BUT THEIR NUMBERS DWINDLE THIN,

WHILE THE SINISTER BATHE IN CONQUEST.

WRITTEN BY JAKE MASTAR
ART BY PEDRO PEREZ
EDITED BY OLIVER GRAY

HERE IT COMES...

SLIDE

TWIRL

IMPRESSIVE.

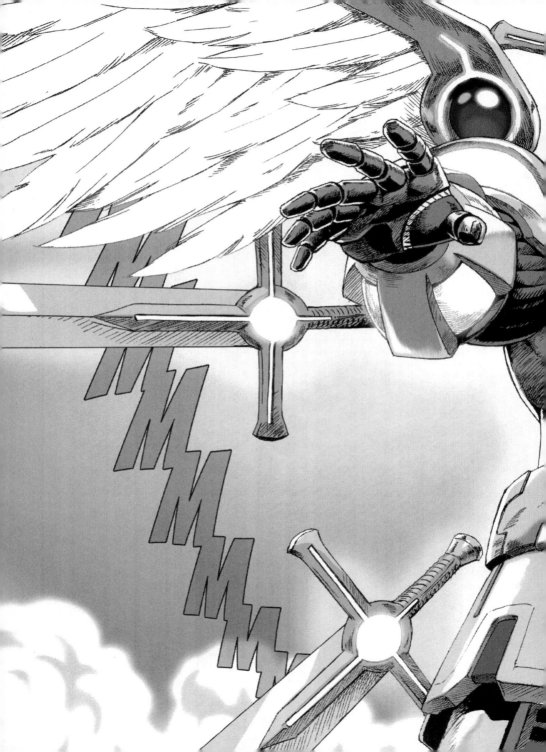

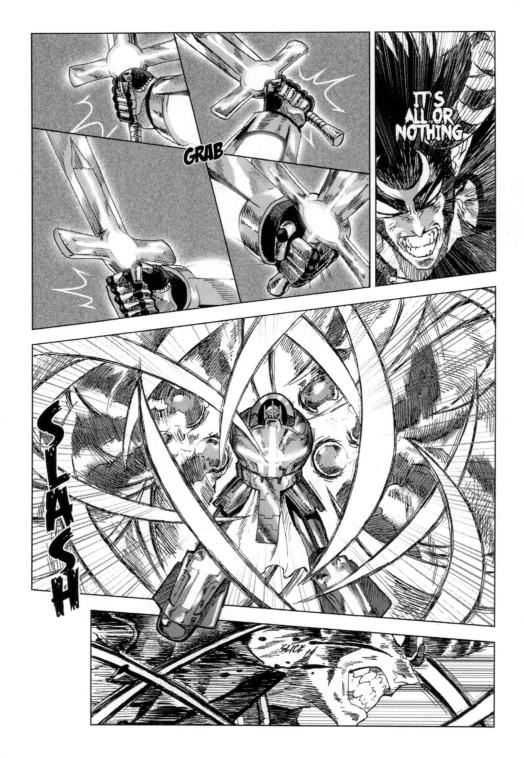

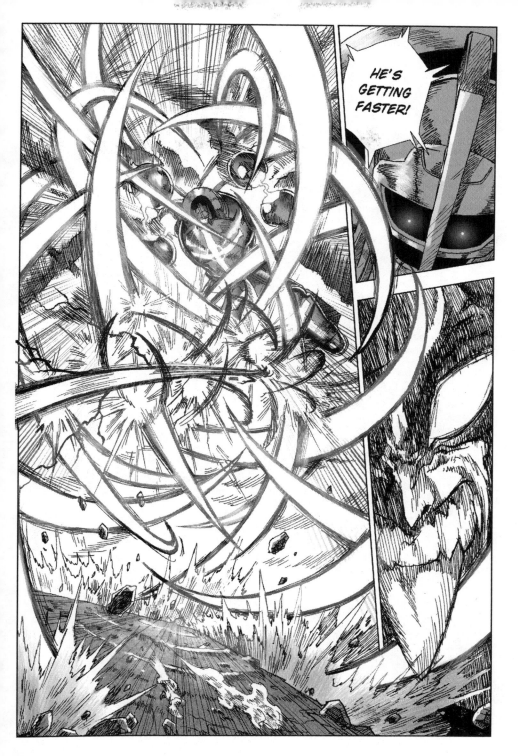

FSSSH##

THUD

HMMM?...

ONE OF THE *RAPHAELIAN* ARTIFACTS?

NO MATTER, IT ENDS NOW, REGARDLESS.

GASP

WHAT KIND OF FOOL WOULD CHALLENGE THE ANGEL OF DESTRUCTION.

DEMONS GET MORE BRASH EVERY MILLENNIA.

COUGH

TURN

FHSSSSS

LET ME TAKE OVER FOR YOU... BETROTHED ONE

WHAT DEVILRY IS THIS?

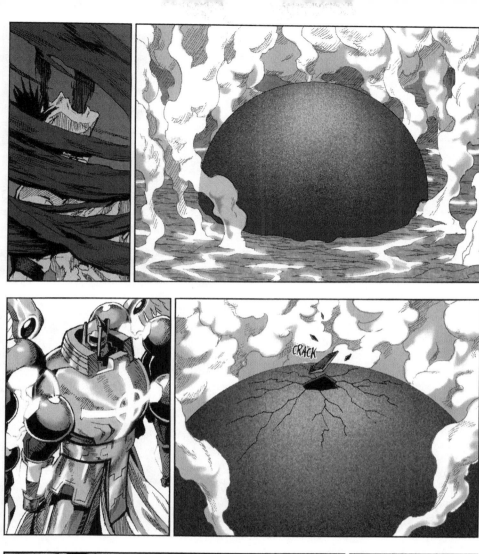

CRACK

AIM

FHOOOSS

THE GREAT-
SWORDS OF
DESTRUCTION
......?!

OMNI POTENS

FERRUM

LUCIFER

ONLY ONE ANGEL REMAINS, SOREN. THAT "CASSIEL" YOU ARE SO FOND OF IS MY FINAL TARGET.

AFTER I DESTROY YOU BOTH, IT'S THE END OF THE HOLY KNIGHTS, AND THE **HEAVENLY REALM** WILL CLOSE FOREVER...!

BA BOO

SLAM

!

REVEAL YOURSELF, DEMON!

YOU

THE ONE WHO HAS SLAIN
SO MANY OF MY CHILDREN
YOU'RE TOO LATE, TEMPLAR..
THE "ASCENSION" IS NIGH.
I'M GOING TO FIND A WAY TO DESTROY YOU, *LUCIFER*!.

PAIN

FATHER!

KRAKOOM

SOON ENOUGH
YOU WILL FACE
MY FULL POWER.

MAGNA
DAEMONIUM
VIM...

LIFT

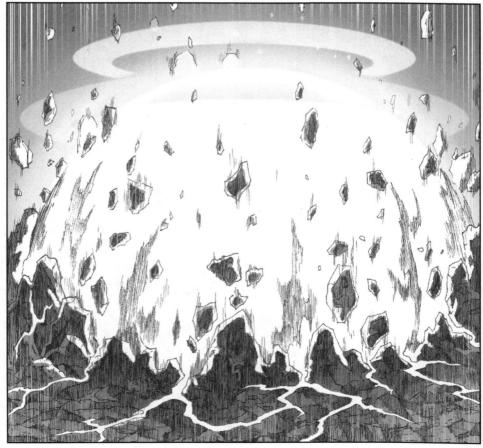

DEMONRUSH: CHAPTER 1 –*END*

Made in the USA
Las Vegas, NV
24 September 2023

78099005R00046